KT-548-056

Beyond the Shining Water

'Now give over,' he told her firmly. 'I'll be home in three or four weeks time …'

'But three or four weeks is *forever*, Liam,' she wailed.

'No, it isn't. Now just get this date in your head, May the fourteenth, got it, an' every day after that you come down here an' see if I've arrived. About the same time. Now cheer up and give us a smile …'

She put her arms about his waist and buried her face in the middle buttons of his shirt, hugging herself close to him and without thought he stroked her silky hair and murmured some soft endearment before turning away and striding off down the beach.

She watched him go, her childish face wet with tears for it was like those days when Pa had left them, her and her Ma, both of them bereft without him.

Also by Audrey Howard in Coronet Paperbacks

The Mallow Years
Shining Threads
A Day Will Come
All the Dear Faces
There is No Parting
Echo of Another Time
The Woman from Browhead
The Silence of Strangers
A World of Difference
Promises Lost
The Shadowed Hills
Strand of Dreams
Tomorrow's Memories
Not a Bird Will Sing
When Morning Comes

About the author

Audrey Howard was born in Liverpool in 1929 and it is from that once great seaport that many of the ideas for her books come. Before she began to write she had a variety of jobs, among them hairdresser, model, shop assistant, cleaner and civil servant. In 1981, out of work and living in Australia, she wrote the first of her twenty-one published novels. She was fifty-two. Her fourth novel, *The Juniper Bush*, won the Boots Romantic Novel of the Year Award in 1988. She now lives in her childhood home, St Anne's on Sea, Lancashire.

The ght the work

C

First publishe

First publish

All rights
reproduce
in any fo
permission
in any form
it is pub
in

All characters in t
real per

A CIP

Pr